CW01065053

LITTLE WARRIOR

LITTLE WARRIOR

Written By
Natalie Aghyarian
Illustrated by Noel Mazmanian

Little Warrior

First Edition

Paperback ISBN: 979-8-8229-1481-0
Hardcover ISBN: 979-8-8229-2997-5

To my son:

You are my love.

You are my light.

You are the reason this book came to life.

I love you.

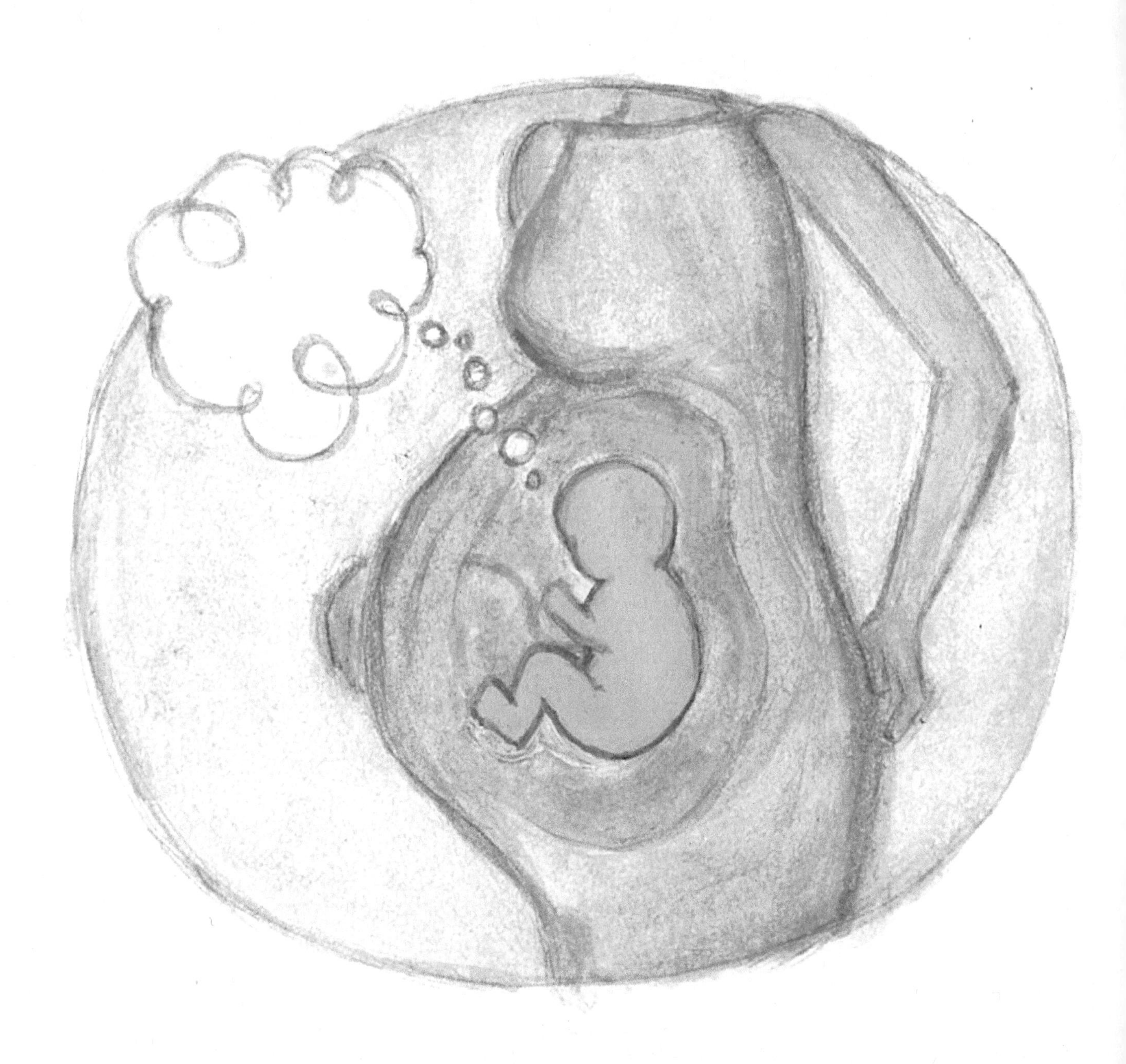

When I was in Mommy's tummy,
I would always dream
about my life and what
Mommy and Daddy looked like.

When I was in Mommy's tummy,
I kicked, I rolled, I yawned,
I hiccupped, I ate, and I slept.

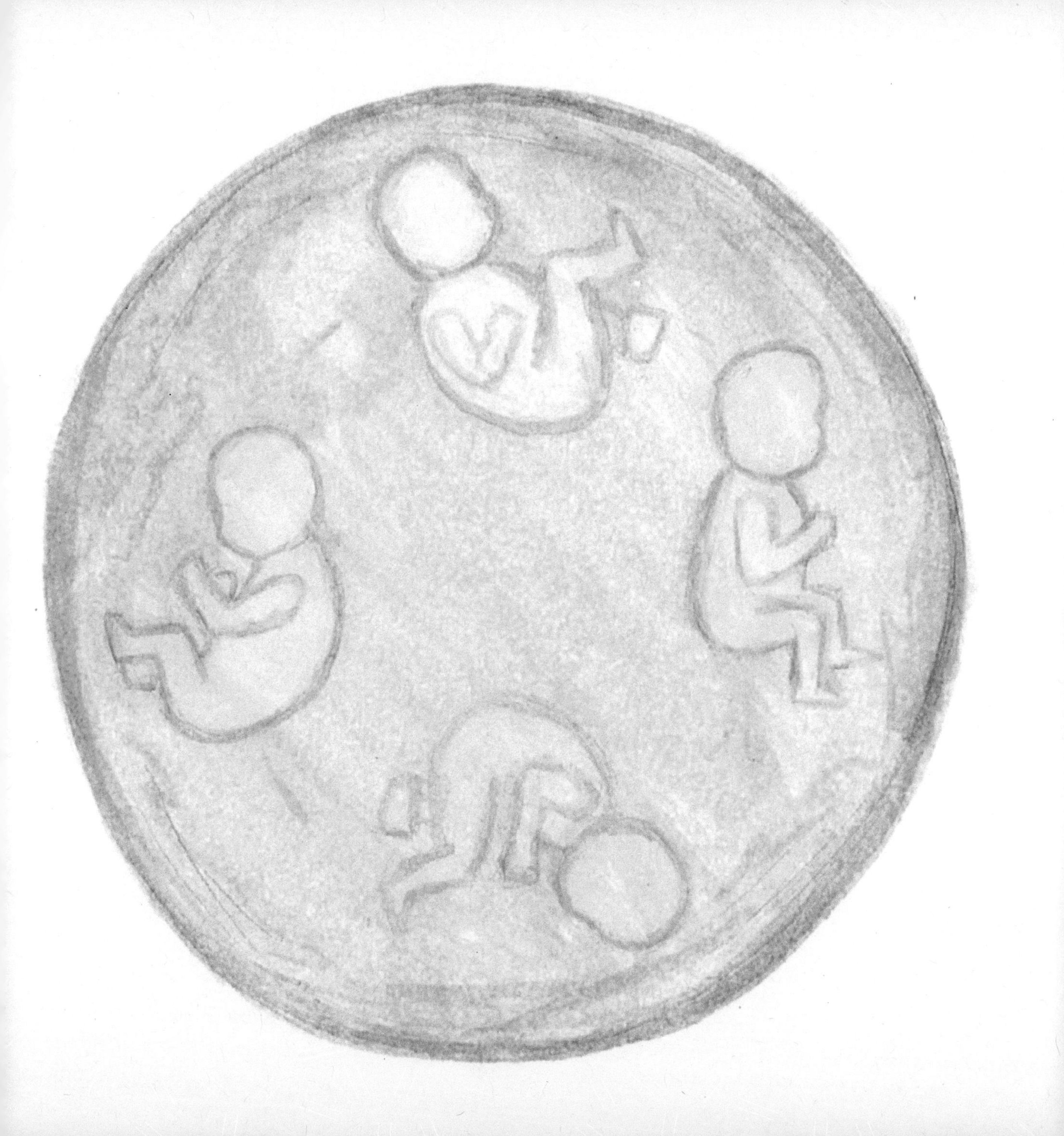

When I was in Mommy's tummy,
I connected with Mommy
in the most special way.

When I was in Mommy's tummy,
I heard so many different noises
and could hear
Mommy's heartbeat and voice.

Then the day was here,
and it was time for me
to make my appearance.

A FEW SCARY THINGS
HAPPENED ALONG THE WAY,
BUT WITH A LOT OF HELP
FROM DOCTORS,

Mommy, Daddy, and
the rest of my family,
we got through it!

So, whenever I have a bad day,
I remind myself just how amazing
and strong I am.
Mommy looks at me and says,
"I just knew you were a little
warrior, even in Mommy's belly."

W

A WARRIOR

IS JUST WHAT I AM.

Milton Keynes UK
Ingram Content Group UK Ltd.
UKHW050242241023
431213UK00003B/8